ICHTHYIC

IN THE

AFTERGLOW

For

by Jason Wayne Allen

For my wife,

Melissa Allen

The Clown turned his powdered face to the mirror:

"If to be fair is to be beautiful," he said, "who can compare with me in my white mask?"

"Who can compare with him in his white mask?" I asked Death beside me.

"Who can compare with me?" said Death, "for I am paler still."

"You are very beautiful," sighed the Clown, turning his powdered face from the mirror."

— Robert W. Chambers,
The King in Yellow and Other Horror Stories

Chapter One

CLEM HELD HIS BREATH INSIDE THE SUICIDE CHAMBER. His eyes stung in the haze of yellow gas, needles on gauges reached the red. He was a breath away from dying when cowardice prevailed.

Clem pressed the cancel button on the control panel, frantically pried the door open, and bailed out. He rolled onto the concrete, coughing violently. The crowd gathered outside the suicide chamber was a diverse collection, ranging from housewives to gutter punks, the terminally ill, body builders, the wheelchair bound, and fresh faced teenagers lined the block. Everyone wanted to die and suicide chambers had recently become affordable, every sector in the Imperiam had a black skull at its center.

Clem looked up and glaring down from above was a middle-aged man, balding, in a dress shirt, and tie decorated with Christmas reefs. "Are you finished?" Clem nodded. The middle-aged man fed dollar bills to the black skull. The chamber's teeth parted and the middle-aged man stepped inside.

Clem cursed himself for wasting his rent money on the suicide chamber. Of course, there were no refunds. He would have to visit his father and ask for a loan.

He contemplated jumping in with the middle-aged man before the black skull closed its teeth. There were two security guards in the black skull's eyes, on the second tier, they would just shut down the machine, and have him thrown in jail for trying to steal a suicide.

Clem got to his feet. Dramatic gasping, heckling, and laughter came from the crowd gathered around the suicide chamber as inhuman screams mixed with delirious laughter came from the middle-aged man dying inside. The method of suicide Clem chose was gas, because he figured it would be the least painful, it sounded like the middle-aged man chose bludgeoning. Clem figured next time he'd have to suck it up, and choose a more brutal method. Nothing worth doing is ever easy, death was no different.

Another purple day under a cancerous sun, in the afterglow of a world that was and will never be again. Clem made his way past a variety of prostitutes and other solicitors, offering jewelry, food, sex, and some just simply asking for money.

"Hey fish boy," said a fat, hairy, topless transvestite in a gimp mask and plaid skirt. "You wanna tap this? Tightest ass in the Imperiam?"

"What's up, Tina," said Clem. "Not today, I'm kind of strapped for cash." The transvestite didn't reply and gave the same offer to the next guy.

"You got a dollar?" asked a young pregnant girl with empty eye sockets and pink hair.

"No money sorry, Chloe," said Clem. "If I had anything, I'd give it to you."

Indifferent, Chloe asked the next guy.

On the curb outside Clem's apartment building, a nude,

emaciated man with no arms played country blues on an acoustic guitar with his feet. "...*your Southern can belongs to me (in the mornin'), your Southern can belongs to me...,"* he sang.

"What's up, Mac?" said Clem. Mac looked over and nodded at Clem, without missing a note.

Clem got inside his apartment. Flies clouded and mingled in the stink of stale beer, rotting garbage, and dog shit. Chico scurried into the room barking and baring his teeth until he realized it was Clem. "Settle down, killer. Who's a good boy," Clem baby-talked and picked the Chihuahua up. "Who's hungry?" Chico vibrated with excitement in his arms.

Dogs were as rare as angels these days. Clem happened upon Chico a few months back after his first failed visit to a black skull.

In an alley that evening, three robed and hooded, Ultharian cultists in rubber cat masks genuflected around the little guy. He cowered, shaking in the center of a Star Claw sigil scrawled with chalk. Black marble eyes met Clem's own. Clem generally minded his own business, but he couldn't ignore the Chihuahua. "Hey," Clem shouted. Each cultist turned eerily, simultaneously. "That's my dog," Clem choked, timid. The three figures walked slowly toward him. "I'll get a policeman!"

Ultharian cults had cropped up in the Imperiam in recent years and dog sacrifice was a felony. These three cultists didn't seem to care. Clem's leg came out from under him and things blinked on and off when his head bounced off the pavement. He curled into the fetal position as feet and fists rained down. In the distance the dog squeaked furious barks. When Clem came to, wallet gone—no worries there, it was empty anyway— and pockets turned out, the Chihuahua was licking his face.

After Clem fed Chico, he got ready for work. He put on a white shirt with black stripes, pulled his pants high above his waist, and snapped on suspenders. Before he put on the greasepaint he studied his face in the mirror.

His thirties had not been kind to him. His hair had long ago fallen out, he seemed to lose a tooth every week, and his mouth pulled into a constant frown. Clem's more ichthyic features were becoming more prominent. Soon enough, he would be a fish.

His ears had fallen off last year and he hated his artificial ones, he snapped them on and smoothed his hand over his cheeks and peeled flaking skin. He turned the water on in the sink and washed his face, every time he washed his face the scales developing glowed grayish-gold under what was left of his human skin.

He applied make-up thick on his face, circled black eyeliner around his eyes. The final touch was the slightly cocked beret'. He made a terribly ugly person, but a handsome mime.

Being a mime was not dependable work. He could show up at *Whosit Whosit Party Corp.* and there could be no jobs available. There were hundreds of workers vying for gigs, and they all got up early in the morning and reported for duty. Clem had gotten up early, but of course chose the suicide chamber instead of simply reporting for work.

Clem looked at himself in the mirror and sighed. There was no way around it; he'd have to visit his father for a loan.

The Colonel would not be happy with him. Not that he ever has been.

"Okay boy," Clem said. "I'll be back later on. Hopefully old lady Cranston won't come knocking today, demanding her money. You be a good boy." The Chihuahua wagged his tail.

Clem made his way into the late purple morning, and sighed at the new dead day.

Chapter Two

PURPLE LIGHT INVADED CASSIE'S BEDROOM, her face furrowed in a grimace. She wore a large Ramones t-shirt, panties, and on both sides of her as she lay sprawled in her posh bed, sitting sentinel, two giant stuffed polar bears in gas masks. She grumbled, ran her hands up her face and through her chin-length green hair, and heaved her pregnant belly to the other side of the bed.

"Rise and shine, sweetheart. Today's the big day."

Cassie moaned. "Huh? Daddy? When did you get back?"

"Earlier this morning." Cassie's father had been on a business trip. Doctor Syndrome was a renowned plastic surgeon and was always away.

"What's so big about today," Cassie said, annoyed.

"You're getting an abortion."

"Like hell," said Cassie, suddenly sitting up. "I've carried this baby almost to term. And daddy, it has not been easy."

"Where's the father?" said Doctor Syndrome, arms crossed looking down at his daughter.

Cassie wondered this herself. She had not spoken with Carl since she told him she was pregnant and every time she called him his phone went straight to voice mail. She figured she probably dropped a bomb on him announcing the pregnancy and he was just getting his head straight. Then again she feared Lee, Carl's conjoined twin, convinced him to run away and avoid her.

Carl and Lee were from the Carp District and that made Carl that much more appealing. The typical bad boy from the wrong side of the tracks. Her father would *hate* him, but Lee had been a problem since their first and last rendezvous.

Lee made comments, calling her a stuck-up bitch, a little virgin, and Cassie was a virgin when she and Carl first had sex. Cassie had been saving her virginity, but one day she had pulled into a service station to gas up her pink Hello Kitty hover car, and there he was standing outside in a black leather jacket running a comb through his pompadour. She locked eyes with him as she walked inside. Those dreamy blue eyes. The grotesque little head on his shoulder blew raspberries at her.

"Yo, babe," Carl stopped her. "You want to buy some 'Dalos? Good prices."

"Sure," said Cassie, in a confident tone as if she had done 'Dalos before.

She asked if he would do some lines with her. They climbed into Cassie's Hello Kitty hover car, drove into the Carp District and chopped some up on the dash.

There, they watched the cancerous sun set and change the day from purple to pitch. Cassie's first trip into the fourth dimension, stoned to the gills on 'Dalos, in the pink interior light, Cassie gave her virginity to Carl.

During the sex, Lee heckled, "Aw, sick dude. Her tits are wall-eyed. Ha! You two pump chump," on and on.

A few weeks later Cassie found out she was pregnant.

"Look at you," said Doctor Syndrome. "My baby girl has green hair."

"Daddy, I'm almost eighteen. I can dye my hair whatever color I want."

"The operative word there, my dear, is "almost". Go to the bathroom and shave your head, right now. I'm going away later this afternoon; your mother has a very important performance.

I'm not sure when I'll be back, but when I do come back I better see your belly deflated, and that beautiful red hair coming back in."

"But daddy!" Cassie whined, tears welled in her eyes.

"Shave it now, this instant and if you don't get that abortion, I'll perform it myself. I seriously doubt you want your daddy seeing your hoo-ha!"

"You're not even a real doctor," screamed Cassie.

She was right. Doctor Syndrome was not a real doctor. He'd never gotten his license officially, because he couldn't pass the math portion of the final test in college. He supported himself in his younger days by selling 'Dalos, that when snorted in large amounts destroyed the user's nose, like corrosive acid.

One of his buyers was a young, red-haired starlet named Camilla Mahoney. Mahoney had sent a fat line of 'Dalos into her nostril that took her nose with it into the nasal cavity. Before Miss Mahoney choked to death on the back drip of her own nose, Syndrome performed the Heimlich. Using the tools left over from his college days, reconstructed her nose back to its original form. Camilla was so thankful she recommended Syndrome to all the stars. Syndrome gave up dealing drugs and wound up impregnating Camilla, and became a father.

Syndrome was completely ignorant when it came to numbers. It was a crippling embarrassment. He hated his daughter, or anyone knew about this weakness.

"What's twelve times twelve?" said Cassie, defiantly.

Syndrome growled. "Now, young lady, get your ass in there and shave that green shit off of your head, then get to the clinic!"

Cassie stood in front of the bathroom mirror and

sobbed as she sheared her green locks. She would visit a black skull; kill herself, which would show him.

Cassie decided she had to find Carl instead. She would tell him what her father was making her do and he would run away with her. She would leave the Imperiam, maybe move to the Carp District and start a family…but first she had to find Carl.

Chapter Three

STANDING IN LINE BEHIND A MOTHER AND A CRYING child waiting for his turn in the suicide chamber, Melvin adjusted his pants, and made sure the bomb strapped to his chest was still there. This was going to hurt, sure, but he would still have eight more lives to go.

Melvin was a relatively new member of the Calico Militia having joined a couple months back after his father gave up booze for religion. He stopped beating his wife and son, and forced them to join the Order of Nosarii. Worship at the Kennel on Sunday, read the scriptures every evening before bed, mandatory. Melvin had to get away and had heard rumors about a group of Ultharians calling themselves the Calico Militia setting up camp near the Carp District. The group stood against everything his father believed. Nosariis were dogs, the militias were cats—a Satan to his father's God.

Melvin did not go home immediately after school one day and decided to go check it out. The camp was everything Melvin could ask for. Inside the giant warehouse that constituted the campsite, young men and women, wearing rubber cat masks, played video games, pinball, and there was a large vert ramp for skateboarding, (Melvin was a skater and the vert ramp closed the deal).

Camp Calico wasn't all fun and games. The leader of the Calico Militia was Elder Talon, an old Samurai from days passed. He sat upon a throne of rats and wore the mask of a fat orange tabby. By Elder Talon's side, Nip and Fang. Two figures, a male and female in black, Siamese cat masks-- both sleek, with bright green eyes. As well as target practice and weapons, the young recruits were trained in an ancient, esoteric form of martial art called, *Bastetki-Do.*

They were made to file their teeth to points as well as their finger and toenails, shimmy fast up trees, and match the agility and strength of the feline as best they could, given their humble humanoid bodies. The warriors trained hard. War was on the horizon.

A volunteer was needed for the first attack. A meeting was held where the crowd, on their knees, bowed while Elder Talon presided over and spoke of prophecy.

"And who my children," he said in broken English, "will be the one to throw the first stone? Who will be the first to flex his claws in the name of our Ultharian masters?"

Melvin got to his feet. "I will."

"Good boy, step up." Melvin walked up and knelt before the throne of rats and genuflected before Elder Talon. Elder Talon, old and feeble, stretched a rubber mask over the boy's head. The mask was similar to Elder Talon's tabby mask, but a kitten. "You have done your sect proud, boy. And worry not, because it will be just one life lost out of your nine."

"I would give all nine in the name of Ulthar," said Melvin.

Elder Talon let go a hardy laugh. "Ambitious! Haha! Boys and girls, students of my militia, you could all learn from our dear Melvin here. You will go far, son."

Melvin's insides felt fuzzy at the word 'son'. He thought of his father, the fat drunken bastard. The hypocrite. His father believed in nothing. Melvin determined to go far in the Militia. Melvin determined to see his mother out of her circumstance. If he had to kill his father in the process, then so be it.

Melvin was gaining his turn in line to the suicide chamber. The large black skull came closer and Melvin started getting nervous, took a deep breath, and let it go. He had to go through with this; he would see the prophecy flower. He would do the Master proud and his mother.

Melvin looked into the crazed eyes of an infant wailing on its mother's shoulder. The mother and child stepped up and fed dollar bills to the black skull. The black skull's teeth parted. The mother and child stepped inside.

Screams came from inside, normal agonized screams mixed with terror, and then screams like a tape being rewound as vocals chords were ripped and torn.

Then silence.

The crowd outside the suicide chamber gave a massive cheer. Melvin gulped, this would hurt but he would still have eight more lives he told himself. He fed dollar bills to the black skull and its teeth parted. Melvin stretched the rubber cat mask over his face and turned to the crowd behind. "For the Calico Militia! For Ulthar!"

The teeth parted and Melvin stepped inside the black skull.

•••

"...The remains of the attacker have been identified as Melvin Grossman, age seventeen. A member of the Calico Militia, one of many Ultharian based religious cults that have sprung up in the Imperiam in recent years. There have been rumors of religious sects combining forces and putting denominational differences aside to wage war on these feline worshiping cults. This was the largest attack on the Imperiam in recorded history.

The attack happened earlier this afternoon when Grossman stepped inside a lethal chamber with a bomb strapped to his chest. Grossman is responsible for the deaths of hundreds and counting, the annihilation of a city block, and many businesses. The government who builds these black skull lethal chambers is particularly angry, with profit margins dropping drastically in just an hour, since the attack dealt so much free death..."

"You hear that, boy?" said the Colonel. He lowered the volume on the television. "War. Now you won't have to dress like a prissy mime anymore, and you can serve the Imperiam like I did when I was your age. Best thing that ever happened to me."

There were no jobs available at Whosit Whosit Party Corps. Clem saw it fitting to show up in his mime garb, proof to the Colonel he did, in fact, have a job and could repay him. Before he could ask for the loan, his father shushed him and turned up the volume on the television.

He had heard the blast outside on his walk to his father's. Clem thought it might have been thunder in the distance, but worry came over him when he realized he might not have an apartment to go back to. He hoped Chico was okay.

"And why are you here anyway? Ha! Ha! Do the rope-pull bit," said the Colonel.

"Dad, I'm really not..."

"Do it!" This was the first time he had seen his son in full costume. Clem pantomimed pulling a large rope. The Colonel chuckled.

"Let me guess, you need money? Too bad. I told you to join the military. Serve the Imperiam and the Imperiam would help you out, but you never listened. Now there might be a war. They'll draft you."

"Dad, I think I'm too old," said Clem.

"Bullshit! You're never too old to serve. How old are you anyway?"

"Thirty-two," said Clem. "And aren't we descended from Y'ha-nthlei? We have nothing do with a war between felines and K-9s, we're fish!"

"Those cat bastards are sick. If the dogs need an ally they can count on us! Anyway, I'm not giving you any money. You'll have to join the army."

"Dad, I'll be homeless!"

"You should have listened to me from the start and joined after high school. Now, do the box!"

Clem pantomimed being trapped inside an invisible box. His father clapped and laughed.

Clem supposed if his apartment building was still standing he would be evicted. He and Chico, homeless.

•••

Shock waves from the blast careened the Hello Kitty hover car into the side of a McDonald's Play Place ball pit and caught fire. Cassie's face slammed into the steering column. A gout of blood splashed the windshield from her broken nose. She briefly lost consciousness, came to and spit curses at the children that weren't dead writhing on the flaming hood.

"The fuck off my car!" She opened the driver's side-door and wedged out her pregnant belly. She started flinging limp and crying children off of the car. The flames started spreading to the roof.

Suddenly, she lost gravity and was under someone's arm being carried through the plastic balls.

Before she started to protest, thinking of the Hello Kitty

hover car she was leaving behind, she somehow recognized the yellow robe. *No way,* Cassie thought.

Her head bounced off the concrete. The figure draped the tattered robe over her.

The Hello Kitty hover car exploded. The flames scorched the robe to tatters and blisters birthed on Cassie's back. The figure in the yellow robe helped her to her feet. The figure was wearing a ghastly white featureless mask that cocked curiously as it surveyed Cassie.

"I'm okay," Cassie's voice quivered. "I think I'm okay. The mask nodded. Cassie gasped. The figure faded before her eyes, dematerialized into the aether. Cassie briefly lost herself and the memory of the figure in the tattered yellow robe faded.

Her first thought when she regained composure was, *Daddy will be buying me a new car!*

Screams in the streets. Panic came from all around. Cassie walked on, oblivious.

A helpless cloud came over her. She needed to find Carl. She hoped Carl was okay. She just wanted to cuddle up with him alone, away from all this. Away from the world.

Her, Carl, and the baby...and Lee, who she hoped Carl would get surgically removed. If not she would accept and love Lee because he was a part of Carl. And Carl would accept and love the baby, because it was a part of them.

Carl lived about two miles away. After months of debating showing up unannounced, Cassie decided to make her way to his home, on foot.

She wiped the blood from her face with the tail of her Ramones t-shirt, pulled it back over her swollen belly, and staggered to the Carp District.

Chapter Four

SOMETIMES CLEM FANTASIZED ANTI-MIRACLES. His bank exploding and no more overdraft fees. In high school, long elaborate fantasies would sail him to sleep regarding dead bullies, fires, and all those that laughed at him at his maniacal whim.

The thought of his apartment building reduced to rubble in the wake of that bomb and somehow Chico surviving, climbing from the rubble to greet him. With his apartment building destroyed, wouldn't there be some kind of government shelter?

Clem sighed. The building stood.

"What's up, Mac?" Clem said to the guitar playing amputee.

Mac didn't miss a note. "*Your Southern can belongs to me...*"

Chico greeted him inside.

"Well, boy. It looks like we have to start packing. Cranston will be by soon to collect."

Clem unraveled a plastic garbage bag and stuffed clothes that littered the floor inside. Tears welled as he thought of himself and Chico curled in a dumpster. Destitute, unable to even buy food for his best friend. At least they would starve to death together.

Soon came quickly and three knocks pounded the door, startling Clem and sending Chico into a riot of barking. The doorknob jiggled. Before Clem turn the knob the door flung open, slamming into his face.

A hulking figure in a Siamese cat mask was straddling his chest, pinning his arms to the floor. A cocked fist came down, and Clem thought of his remaining teeth.

"You will not be getting your deposit back," an elderly woman's voice sing-songed. "And will you look here, a dog!" She went to pick Chico up, he snapped at her, his hair rose, and teeth bared. "Vicious little bastard."

"You have been squatting in my building for what, Mr.

Castaigne? Two months now? Do you have my money?"

Cranston was wearing a Siamese cat mask as well, and the sheer night gown she seemed to always be wearing. Clem tried turning his head to her, but Thok held his chin firm, a massive fist at the ready. "No, ma'am, I need more time..."

"Son, show him what we think of squatters who keep pets—especially dogs, without paying a deposit!"

"What is he supposed to be anyway, ma?" Some kind of clown?" Thok chuckled.

"A mime actually..." said Clem.

Thok's massive fist came down. There was a penny-taste of blood, then blackness.

Chapter Five

CASSIE TOOK IN THE DILAPIDATED MOBILE HOMES, and grimaced at the rotten egg-sulfur smell that dominated the Carp District. D*addy would flip if he knew I was here!* She thought. The sparse locals that passed her on the sidewalks stared, mouths gaping and fish-eyed.

The people of the Carp District were notorious for their use of 'Dalos and it showed. Most were mutated from birth and born addicted. An emaciated cyclops with no arms put his stump on Cassie's shoulder.

"Do you have a dollar?" It gurgled.

"Ew! No," said Cassie.

She had run a search online for where Carl lived months ago. The information was saved on her phone, letting it guide her way. The people search website charged significantly extra to find Carl's whereabouts because the Carp District couldn't be found on any published map.

The day had gone from purple to maroon, and pitch would be here soon. She passed a derelict general store with a crooked sign that read '*WE SELL WORMS*'. The digital display on her cell phone indicated she was getting close.

In front of the trailer was a mass graveyard. Makeshift crosses and headstones sprouted from overgrown grass. *A pet cemetery*? She waded through the yard, stepped up on the rickety porch, and knocked. The door slit open revealing a hunched elderly woman's face.

"What?"

"I'm here for Carl," Cassie's voice slightly trembled. "Is he here?" The door opened all the way. A frail old crone in a black robe rolled a wheelchair onto the creaking porch.

"You're swollen. Did Carl and Lee do that to you?" her voice was diaphanous.

"Well," said Cassie rubbing her belly, "Mostly Carl," she giggled nervously.

"I hate to tell you miss," said the crone. "Carl and Lee ain't coming back."

"Where is he? Is he okay?"

"He's alive, as far as I know, miss, but far from okay. I tell you though ol' Carl and Lee are gone for good."

"Do you know where they are?"

"Not exactly," the crone took a breath. "Lee kept talkin' 'bout a place by the name of Carcosa? Think they ran off there. You know it?"

"No ma'am."

"A few months back Carl and Lee got arrested. Some ol' undercover busted the boys selling 'Dalos outside a middle school 'cross the tracks. Did three months in county," the crone chuckled. "Wouldn't the first time ol' Carl and Lee get busted on a 'Dalos charge? Me and the boys father, rest his soul, had bailed the boys out three times at least for sellin' when they's in high school. Anyway, we couldn't get angry with 'em. The family's been selling 'Dalos for generations and the boys always pitched in, helped the family and whatnot...money-wise, I mean.

"Any who, the three months they's in county ol' Lee read a book—Lee's always been the brains of that outfit—called...well, miss I don't quiet remember the exact name, but from what Lee went on and on about, the book was some sorta Bible that talked about a Yellow King that emperors worshiped. Something about a white mask...a pallid *mask!* That's it! Pallid was the word. It was crazy devil worship ya ask me." The crone harked and spat off the side of the porch. "Anyways miss, I hate to say it but they're gone."

Carcosa? Cassie thought. *Daddy will know where Carcosa is, and he will be buying me a ticket.* The oddest part of Carl and Lee's mother's little anecdote was it rang a vague, far off bell in Cassie's memory. Why did it all sound familiar?

"I hope, missy, you'll be lettin' me see my grand baby when it comes."

"You bet, ma'am," Cassie lied.

"What's your name, anyway?"

"Cassie."

"That wouldn't happen to be short for Cassilda would

it?"

"Yes, ma'am," said Cassie.

"The boys sometimes mentioned a Cassilda, before they ran off" said the crone, brow furrowed.

"Carl mentioned me?" Cassie brightened. "What'd he say?"

"You sure you don't know nothing about Carl and Lee goin' to this Carcosa?"

"No ma'am! This is the first I've heard about it. I swear," said Cassie.

"It ain't no matter, I suppose. Before you take off miss, promise me you'll bring that grand baby next time. The cerebral fluid, you know."

"Cerebral fluid?" said Cassie.

"Look at all them, cain't make 'Dalos without a young-un's brains," the crone raised a gnarled finger at the mass graves. Not a pet cemetery, *baby graves,* Cassie thought.

"Don't you know nothin'? With the boys being gone, we

ain't been able to make much 'Dalos. The old man, the boy's father's been dead years now."

*Was she saying they made drugs from the cerebral fluid of babies? And that's why she wants to see her grandchild?*The thought disgusted Cassie.

"Yeah, I'll bring the baby sometime" said Cassie, backing down the porch steps, appeasing the old woman until it was safe to run.

Chapter Six

*"...**THIS, MY BROTHERS AND SISTERS, IS A TESTAMENT** to our ability to recover, to rebuild. And through tragedy, come together, defiant of one devil. We will not be intimidated. And as you can all see from the construction already begun, we are told this sector of the Imperiam will have a newly erected lethal chamber by morning..."*

"Fish boy?" Clem was being stirred awake. He licked his teeth to make sure what few he had were all there. Tina was standing above him smoking a cigarette. He had taken off the gimp mask revealing a thick, chest-length beard. The transvestite was nudging him awake with the toe of his stiletto. An ocean of gasps came from the crowd.

"They're building a new black skull," said Tina, exhaling

smoke.

"Already?" Clem clumsily got to his feet. Mrs. Cranston's monster of a bastard son had done a number on him. He licked his split lips.

"They claim they'll have it done by morning, we'll see...sweetheart, I hate to tell ya, but ya look like shit. Who beat ya up?"

"The landlord came to collect payment," said Clem.

"Oh you have a room over at old lady Cranston's? Yeah?" Tina chuckled, "Cranston's a mean ol' bitch. And that son of hers, Thok? He's a monster. So, I take it he just beat ya up threw you in the streets."

"That's exactly what happened," said Clem.

Clem thought of Chico. Cranston has Chico!

"And they took my dog," Clem let go a defeated sigh.

"Your dog? You poor thing," Tina stroked Clem's face, gave a disgusted look at his hand where greasepaint had come away, and wiped it on his skirt.

The speaker at the podium wore a blood-red, flowing robe, and the mask of a black Bull Mastiff.

"By morning, step up, those who wish to cease a wretched existence!"

The crowd packed tight, and let go a deafening cheer. Dusk was approaching and a cancerous sun turned everything an eerie maroon. All would be pitch soon.

Clem thought of Chico. He remembered the rubber Siamese cat mask Cranston was wearing. Sudden panic came over him at the thought of her doing...something to his best friend. He remembered the cultists he'd gotten Chico from. Those Ultharians. The crowd suddenly packed tighter around Clem and Tina. So tight, it was becoming difficult to breathe. Then sudden relief as the crowd dispersed around him, and then screams.

On the podium stood a figure with a Siamese cat mask, an unsheathed sword, and raised high, the severed head of a black Bull Mastiff. The figure pulled the mask above his chin, bared its teeth, filed to fangs. It opened its mouth, tongue lapping at blood that drizzled from the neck stump of the bull mastiff.

The rat-tat-tat of automatic weapons. Stark terror

erupted. Someone was firing into the crowd. Tina grabbed Clem's wrist and ran.

As they ran for safety, Clem thought of what his father said about joining the military. Surely, there would be a war and before he had little to live for, and with the eviction and Chico gone, Clem now had nothing to live for at all.

•••

Chico cowered in a Star Claw sigil. Cats of different breeds circled him, threatening, making sure he stayed. Cranston and Thok, their nude bodies smeared in the others blood, made love by flickering candle light. Thok finished and rolled over, spent. Cranston lit a cigarette.

The fireworks of gunfire outside startled the animals.

"Hear that?"

Thok looked over at his mother.

"Revolution," Cranston sighed smoke. Cranston laughed maniacally and spit into her son's waiting mouth. They embraced in another fit of passion.

•••

Cassie made her way back to the Imperiam, her head submersed in concentration, scouring the internet on her cellphone. Keywords: *Carcosa, Yellow King, Pallid Mask.* The book about the Yellow King had been banned ages ago. Carcosa like the Carp District wasn't on any published map. *No big deal, I got daddy's charge card numbers.*

Cassie's concentration was broken when a large figure in a rubber Doberman mask slammed into her, knocking her to the dirt. "Hey," Cassie screamed, "Watch where the fuck you're going!" The Doberman paid her no mind. Panicked crowds stampeded around her. She got to her feet and dusted off her rear.

Cassie walked on. Oblivious she continued reading about Carcosa on her phone. The place had twin suns...*twins, like Carl and Lee, it's too perfect.*

She hissed when a bullet grazed her arm.

"Motherfucker!" Do you know who my father is?!"

Chapter Seven

TINA'S APARTMENT WAS A HOLE-IN-THE-WALL, lust-nest drenched in sleaze. Sex dominated the one bedroom, slash kitchen, slash bathroom. Assorted gimp masks on mannequin heads. Dildos displayed on tables and dressers, erect like model cyclopean buildings. A sex swing sagged like a giant spider web and center-pieced the room.

Clem sat rigid, slightly bobbing with the motions of the waterbed. Glad to have a place to sleep for the night, but awkward nonetheless. Clem highly doubted he would get much sleep, with all that noise and chaos outside the apartment. Then there was the ever-horny Tina. Clem had avoided sex for thirty-two years, as disinterested and asexual as some breeds of frog. He knew he would have to be on guard tonight. Tina was behind him rubbing his shoulders. Clem felt the bristle of Tina's beard on his neck.

"Sweetie, just settle, relax," Tina whispered. "You're okay; tomorrow's a new purple day."

Clem's plans were to get to a military recruiter first thing in the morning. There was no other option. Maybe it wouldn't be so bad. The Colonel was a war hero. He'd fought to establish the Imperiam. Maybe that would earn Clem some respect by the other soldiers by default. Sure, he was older, weaker, but he was Colonel Castaigne's son! And with the Ultharian's attacking twice in one day, he knew they wouldn't decline his enlistment.

His eyes welled with tears. He would never see Chico again and most likely, Chico was dead.

"Honey, you'll be fine," said Tina. "You're safe, hey!" Tina suddenly got up. Stood up and lifted his skirt, displaying his ass for Clem. "You wanna tap this? Would that make you feel better? Free of charge."

"No thanks," Clem sobbed, bobbing with the turbulence of the waterbed. "I'm sorry. I just miss my dog."

"That does suck, sweetie," said Tina. "And I hate to tell ya, but here in the Imperiam, you'd have better luck finding diamonds in cat shit or even lost Carcosa than you would finding a dog. It's better to have loved and lost than...well, you know the saying."

A blast like close thunder startled Clem and Tina. They stared wide-eyed at a small window with a beaded curtain.

"What are your plans, sweetie?"

"I have no choice," Clem groaned. "I'll have to join the military. At least for once my dad won't be totally ashamed of me."

"Oh, sweetheart," said Tina, adjusting Clem's artificial ears. "You are preaching to the choir about fathers and their shame. My dad not only was ashamed of me, he disowned me, and furthermore put himself and the rest of the family in a sort of witness protection program. The Order of Nosarii paid a pretty penny for someone to repair the family's reputation after his only son came out queer."

"I'm sorry that happened to you," said Clem.

Tina lit a cigarette. "No, sweetie," he exhaled. "I'm lucky

to be alive. The Nosarii's don't play. There was a kiddie-diddler, priest high in the Nosarii ranks. Someone respected. I won't name names. Your typical young boy, priest scandal...you've heard the rumors."

Clem nodded the affirmative.

"Well, that man who would sneak into my room of a night with that Doberman mask...we fell in love. As inappropriate as the relationship was, it blossomed into more than a victim and predator situation.

But, I got stupid. I came out, being the dumb punk that I was. I was set to be executed, but the man in the Doberman mask, my love, saved me, by confessing our relationship. His status in the ranks of the Nosarii was so prestigious they couldn't slander themselves and let the scandal out, so it was suppressed, of course.

A Repairer of Reputations came in and recovered the family name. I was sent to the streets of the Imperiam. I, naturally, took up hooking. And that's that. I sometimes think of my father, my sister, my mother, but that was another life a million miles away. And," Tina exhaled another plume of smoke. "As long as I live I'll never forget the man in the Doberman mask."

Tina leaned into Clem's face, put his hand over his. "My advice, sweetie, is you do whatever you want to do, on your own terms. Sure, it'll be a struggle. Sure, you might even be homeless here in the Imperium, forced to sling your ass for cash like me, but even if you go down alone, and miserable, you'll at least go down on your own terms. Don't join your father's army."

The gunfire and rumble of bombs got closer.

"Do with your life, what you, and only you deem best."

The beads on the window rattled and a sheathing sound cut the air.

Tina's face lost substance, eyes rolled, and his head fell into Clem's lap. The stray bullet had taken the back of Tina's head. Clem sat for seconds in paralyzed shock staring at the fractured skull and exposed brain. He pushed the head from his lap.

Clem slung open the door of Tina's sex den and made his way into the hall, determined to do what he failed to do that morning.

Chapter Eight

CAMILLA LAUGHED, COUGHED, AND SPAT BLOOD as a figure in a white mask and yellow hooded robe with a dagger, sawed from her groin to gullet. She laid stark nude on a slab of red and black checker board. Doctor Syndrome stood in line, completely ignorant to numbers he had no idea if his turn would come sooner or later. He felt his cell phone vibrate in his pocket. The display read: 'Cassilda'. He raised the white mask, annoyed. He answered.

"I hope you're calling to tell me you got the abortion."

"Nope and I'm not getting it either," said Cassie. "But, I'll make you a deal..."

"I am not negotiating this, young lady. Get your ass to the clinic!"

"Listen daddy. Please daddy, listen." She broke into soft baby talk. Syndrome melted.

"Okay, what is your proposal? Wait, just a second." The orchestra in the background swelled with pure din. Not a hint of melody or anything resembling music. Syndrome made his way to an antechamber.

"Okay. What?"

"What was that?" said Cassie. "Are you at a party?"

"Yes," said Syndrome. "Your mother gave a great performance tonight. After being out of work so long! Camilla Mahoney—your mother, dear, is back! It was a huge deal, the crew is celebrating. Now, what is it?"

"I'm keeping my baby. Get me to Carcosa, that's where Carl is, and I'll leave you and mom alone forever. You won't hear a peep out of me."

Syndrome sighed. "Dear, you have never wanted for anything. I've never really put my foot down about anything, but I can not allow you to have this baby. Your mother's family is part of a...bigger plan, it's hard to explain. This baby will mess up the order. You said the father is in Carcosa?"

Sobs from Cassie. "Yes, daddy. I want to be with Carl! I want to go to Carcosa!"

Laughs from Syndrome. "Dear. You are never going to see Carl again. Trust me. I'm telling you. He chuckled, get the abortion."

"Fuck! You! I hate you," Cassie spat and hung up.

Syndrome shook his head at the phone and chuckled. He put on his mask and walked back into the party.

The orchestra was deafening, violinists and other strings, bled from the mouth as they played with their teeth, and through self-sodomy woodwinds and brass blew.

There was no more line at the checkerboard slab. Camilla Mahoney's body was being removed in pieces by white masked and yellow-robed figures.

A figure pulls Syndrome's mask from his face. Another figure holds out a gold plate with a mini-mountain of yellow powder. Syndrome buries his face in the powder. A figure indicates he strip. Syndrome goes into spasms of laughter, stripped nude, and lay on the checkerboard slab.

As the 'Dalos peaks, Syndrome is ignorant to the

penetration of the dagger. Oblivious as the masked figure reaches inside his stomach and takes out ropes of entrails.

Ignorant to anything outside the fourth dimensional vortex. As ignorant of death as he was to numbers.

Chapter Nine

CRANSTON SAT UP IN BED SMOKING A CIGARETTE. Thok lay next to her snoring. The black and white television flickered light in an otherwise pitch room.

"*...Reports are in that Nosarii forces have neutralized the Ultharians. Earlier, a splinter group of Ultharian terrorists calling themselves the Calico Militia attacked a crowd gathered for the announcement of the Imperiam's new lethal chamber. This is the second attack in one day. The first being when a Melvin Grossman, age seventeen, detonated a bomb this morning inside a black skull suicide chamber. Our sources tell us that The Order and The Nosariis are splitting into vigilante groups, raiding resident's homes, and executing any and all Ultharians without discretion. Terrorists or not...*"

Cranston sent a bony elbow into Thok's snoring face. "Wake up!" Thok moaned and rolled over. "Get up! They are going to be here any minute. We have to take the dog and get to the Carp District. We have to hide out until this blows over."

"Why?" Thok mumbled.

"Because they are raiding houses and killing Ultharians."

"How would they know we're Ultharians?"

"You moron. The sign out front!"

The sign displayed out front read 'Cranston Suites' with a Star Claw sigil shadowing backdrop behind the text. A bullseye.

Cranston shambled out of bed and put her nightgown on. Thok sat up and struggled with socks and boots.

Cranston shoos away the cats surrounding Chico, and scoops him up. He growls in her arm and she spats the dog's face. "Whatever happens, they don't get the dog. And they're here," Cranston split the blinds. Outside a mob of armed figures in assorted dog masks surrounded Cranston's Suites, flashlights breaking the Imperiam's pitch. Cranston looked at

Thok, and nodded. A silent understanding.

The apartment door cracks and splinters as armed Nosariis make their way inside. Thok tackles the first one he sees and pins a Doberman-masked Nosarii to the floor. A blast and Thoks's skull fragments. Brain splatters the wall adjacent. Thok falls over. Cranston lets go a scream.

"Put down the dog!" a muffled voice from a Doberman mask. Cranston holds Chico out by the neck. His tongue lolling from the strangle. The Nosariis raise their rifles. There's no way out but the window. A ten-story drop. She throws Chico at the wall covered in her son's brains, and dives for the window. Blasts from rifles ring with the sound of tinkling glass.

Three Nosariis look down from the shattered window. Their flashlights break the pitch below, and Cranston's frail body is contorted in the street.

A Nosarii picks up the shaken dog. He pulls the Saint Bernard mask over his head. "I've never seen a real one before." The others gather around Chico, petting him. "He has to be one of a kind!"

Another Nosarii removes his mask. "He'll go to the

Kennel, and be dipped in the marble solution."

Chico whimpered.

•••

The Colonel felt defeated and old when reports of the second attack came in. Tears boiled in his bulbous eyes, he ran his hand up and down his scaly head, and prayed.

The Colonel had declined his return to deep Y'ha-nthlei. As a soldier he had defended the Imperiam. He was responsible for establishing the city, and he lived with the guilt of denying his destiny.

He declined flocking with his brethren into the depths of Y'ha-nthlei and standing before father Dagon in all His majesty. Worse he had left pregnant Lavinia still pubescent gold, and ichthyic from the neck down. Her fins prominent at the neck like all young ladies of The Esoteric Order. Her skin golden before gray.

Lavinia his wife. She had died giving birth to the boy, and the Colonel had never truly forgiven him. He tried to love the boy she named Clem. She didn't even bother making him a junior. He had refused to join, and defend his birthright. Pure laziness. The boy was whatever he was because of the Imperiam, and he wouldn't stand up for her? Pathetic. The boy was a clown. Hilarious, yes, but a clown no less.

The guilt haunted the Colonel through the years, but the Imperiam was home. All of his prayers started with pleas of forgiveness.

"I□! I□! Unworthy, on my knees before you Father Dagon! From the depths of Y'ha-nthlei to the depths of my treacherous heart, I beg guidance!" On his knees in his one bedroom apartment, the old fish-headed man went on.

"Y'ha-nthlei, I□! I□! I have declined my destiny to mingle with heathens and mortals. This is true, but Father I beg strength to defend these misguided souls in the name of Y'ha-nthlei!

In the name of Dagon!

Praise Mother Hydra, I beg guidance!"

The prayer stirred his guts, tears sprayed, and in trance the Colonel went into Aklo-spasms, similar to Tongues.

"...Oftu bkda D'khee Y'ha-nthlei Ia! Mother Hydra! I□! I□! Father Dagon..."

Old knees creaked as he got to his feet, and stumbled like a somnambulist to a closet. The door flung open revealing a shrine of ichthyic skulls, and a photo of Father Dagon. The fish god looming monolithic in silhouette.

Prayer meant barter, sacrifice. Any God. To ask without sacrifice...

The Colonel took a ceremonial dagger jeweled at the hilt, and a jeweled diadem.

Back to his knees, he took down his sweatpants, unfurled his flaccid manhood, and started to saw.

"I□! I□!"

He put the diadem on his head, and sawed until the trepidation subsided, sawed until the blood came, and then sawed until the tears came.

"I□! I□!"

Outside the roar of sea: "...I□! I□!"

The knocks came insistent, startling the Colonel. Sweatpants around ankles he stumbled, fumbled with the knob, and opened the door. The limp body of an Ultharian in a Siamese cat mask fell through, twitching. Its hands bound behind him. Two Nosariis entered.

"Sir, you're bleeding."

"What is this?" said the Colonel.

"The Nosariis need your help," The soldier with the mask of a German Shepard leaned down, held out his hand, and hoisted the Colonel to his feet. The soldier noticed the Colonel's crotch fountaining blood, and stepped back. His member dangled on a string of skin. The Colonel winced as he pulled his sweatpants to his waist.

"What's going on?"

"We retaliated immediately after the second attack," said a soldier in the mask of a Chihuahua, "Our own war."

"Has your counter measures been sanctioned by the Imperial Dynasty?"

"No sir," said the soldier. The Colonel sighed.

The soldier reached down and wrenched the rubber mask from the head of the Ultharian.

"He can't be more than fifteen," said the Colonel.

"Exactly. This Calico Militia, we've heard, are seducing kids in as young as ten. It's led by some freak, calls himself, Elder Talon."

"Where is this Elder Talon?" said the Colonel.

"That's why we need your help," said Saint Bernard mask. "We raided Ultharian's homes, tortured their families, and did everything to get them to talk. Some committed suicide before we got to them. Over at Cranston Suites some of our men confiscated a dog."

"What? Some Ultharian piece of shit was hoarding a K-9?" said the Colonel.

"We couldn't believe it either. It's at a Kennel waiting for the marble mixture."

The boy on the floor went into spasms; he writhed like a fish, trying to break his bonds. The three looked at him.

"So, what do you want with me?" said the Colonel.

"This kid is straight from the Calico Militia, look at his teeth," said Chihuahua mask.

The Colonel reached down and pinched open the young man's clenched lips. The boy's terror amplified as the

Colonel got closer.

"Fangs," said the Colonel.

"Exactly," said Saint Bernard mask. "These are extremist orthodox Ultharians. This kid knows where The Calico Militia operates; we need you because of your reputation, but mostly, um your heritage."

The Colonel gave a puzzled look.

Saint Bernard mask sighed. "The Innsmouth look, I believe it's called. These kids think they're fucking cats! We need your intimidation factor...the look!"

The Colonel reached down, grabbed a fistful of the boy's hair, and shook him.

"The base! Where is Talon?" The Colonel pressed his flat nose to the boy's cheek. The boy's swollen eyelids, thick with tears opened slowly, and he panicked seeing the Colonel.

"The fucking base!" The Colonel screamed.

Futility set in and the boy went limp.

"Near Carp. Yellow sector," the boy groaned, like a death rattle. The Colonel let go, and stepped back. The back of the boy's head fell with a thud. Saint Bernard mask reached behind, and leveled his rifle at the boy's head, and fired.

"Seriously?" said the Colonel. "Right here in my living room? You're cleaning this shit up!"

"Sorry sir," said Saint Bernard mask.

"Well, you heard him," said the Colonel. "We are going to the Yellow Sector, and killing these bastards. Call in some more Nosariis."

"We?" said Chihuahua mask.

"Damn right. The Imperiam is my city, and while I don't agree with going over the Imperial Dynasty's head, and taking matters into your own hands, maybe we don't need another war. These assholes can be flushed out quick...and tonight. Right after I see a medic."

Chapter Ten

CLEM FELT HIS WAY THROUGH PITCH. He tripped over debris and potholes, letting memory guide his way to the suicide chamber. He had lived his entire life in the Imperiam, but the city was so war-torn, and through the pitch—nothingness of its dead moon, was like navigating foreign land. "Sorry," he said, bumping into sparse passing bodies.

Ahead, he heard Mac and knew where he was "...*Your Southern can belongs to me...*" That old Blind Willie McTell song, over and over. Mac never missed a note.

Mac, overcoming his disabilities, never letting his lack of arms gets in the way of his passion to play that song until the end of his days had given Clem some vague hope. Hope, but vague, and fleeting nonetheless.

Clem's passion had always been the art of pantomime. It was a lost art, but he enjoyed seeing smiles on those as he mimicked solid air. If only miming brought in some cash. The pressure, so much to live up to. Standards.

He saw Mac, and saw freedom. Freedom was for the brave. Clem didn't have the guts for freedom. He could pursue his passion at Whosit Whosit Party Corp. and in virtual poverty live under a cloud of disappointment with himself and from his father, and live lonely, grow old, and migrate with the few left of his kind to deep Y'ha-nthlei. There was no way that was happening. The migration might be a myth, anyway. The Colonel was still here.

How did Mac live? Did he eat? Sleep? He wasn't a typical panhandler, he never even asked for cash. He just played, day in, day out, driven by...something, maybe supernatural. The elements had long taken the clothes from his back, and Clem could never remember a time Mac was not outside Cranston's Suites playing. He had probably been there since the establishment of the Imperiam.

Chaos all around him that day, and he played on,

oblivious. It seemed if he no longer played, *the Imperiam would be no longer*. Good old Mac, the heart of the city.

Ahead, Clem saw spotlights. A new black skull was to be erected by morning, and from the sound of the jackhammers, and other tools progress was being made.

Clem's plan was to be second in line. Get inside the black skull before it closed its teeth. If the watchmen in the second tier got to him before he got inside he would have to act erratically enough, pose a threat, and hope the guard shoots him.

Anxiety at the thought of this caused Clem's heart to flutter. This would be the boldest move he had ever made in his life. He had never stood up to a bully, a boss, or his father. He would stand up to his life: this futile infliction.

Clem felt his way through, and his hand fell on a face. The face was soft, and his thumbs felt the empty eye sockets. The pregnant belly, it was Chloe. "Do you have a dollar?"

"I'm sorry Chloe, I don't."

Dear Chloe. Beautiful for what she was, pregnant and eye-less, wandered the Imperium seemingly forever, like Mac's song.

Tears started to well as nostalgia, and homesickness at the thought of death came. This endearing feeling, Clem knew too well. This feeling was a defense mechanism he would have to fight. He would keep in mind, Chico was gone.

He reached down, felt concrete, and sat down on the curb. He buried his face in the knees at his chest and cried. He would watch the erection of the new black skull, and be second in line.

Faintly, through the noise of construction a female voice screamed, and sobbed.

Chapter Eleven

LIGHTNING SPIDER-WEBBED CASSIE'S GUTS, she held her belly, and moaned. Two contractions in ten minutes as she made her way to the suicide chamber.

The futility of finding Carl sank in deep when every people search website she emailed inquiring about Carcosa replied: 'HA AH HA HA'...as mockingly as her father. The whole world seemed to be laughing at her. And to live without Carl was simply out of the question.

All of the boys at her school had ignored her because she was fat. They never openly said it, because they feared getting their nose bloodied, but Cassie knew it.

In her Hello Kitty hover car that night in the fourth dimension as the 'Dalos peaked, hounds whimpered, and barked as she gave herself utterly and completely to Carl in the star-lit, windy vortex.

He loved every inch of her. Kissed every inch of her. Her stretch marked breasts, her chubby belly, ran his tongue across the muffin-top of her hips. Lee perched on Carl's shoulder heckled on, but ignored. Forever happened to Cassie that night, and even when forever climaxed inside her and ended, she would forever love Carl...Lee and all. Love him until she stepped inside the suicide chamber, and the madness of love subsided. Forever.

Why was her father so sure she would never see him again? And furthermore what was this play her mother had been in? Camilla hadn't had a job in months. She was well passed her prime as far starlets go, and Cassie couldn't remember a time her mother ever acted in anything besides films. Never an onstage production.

Then all the talk from Carl and Lee's mother about Carcosa, and yellow kings, and her father's mentioning of Carcosa. How come she had never heard of this place until today? This was obviously some kind of conspiracy. Maybe, an elaborate plan by Carl to keep her away. Maybe he was ashamed of her. She had no more want to fight it either. Sick realization reared its head, and Cassie accepted.

After the way her father had denied her, laughed at her, she couldn't imagine facing him again. She would likely kill him, and her mother. They would come back from wherever they were, and she would be gone, and they would be sorry.

Another burst of pain in her guts, and Cassie fell to her knees, doubled-over. Tears came from the intensity of the contractions, her knees on concrete quivering. Through the Imperiam's pitch she sees spotlights, gets to her feet, and walks on. Feeling her way through.

Cassie clenches her teeth as another shot of pain hits. The contractions went from ten minutes apart to two. Sweat broke out on her forehead, she bent and vomited. She regained composure, determined not to slow down, Cassie made her way to the suicide chamber.

Chapter Twelve

Chico shivered in the harness, dangling on a chain. The machine clicked and moaned as he lowered.

At the bottom of the pool fish lay on their sides, roses, limbs, and bodies human and humanoid, forever in the fetal position, or frozen in struggle. Black marble eyes of the Chihuahua quivered and roamed, surveying the men in dog masks.

They looked like him, but was not his brother. They looked more like Clem with his face...similar faces, at least. Not Chico's friends. Not Chico's Clem.

Where was Clem? So hungry. Scared.

Another notch. Lower.

Lonesome.

Harnessed in tight, he whimpers. Licks his muzzle.

Clem, day in. Clem, day out. And day out was the best part.

Tired, Chico would lick Clem's face, the taste like fish. "Who's a good boy?"

Clem would crack another can or open a bottle, and mumble on. About destiny, mumble on about a Dagon, about a Christ, about his father. Chico listened.

Clem said he wanted to die. The pat on the head, scratch behind Chico's ear, Clem equaled home. Then, Clem would sleep, and then Chico would sleep nuzzled in Clem's neck. Chico understood love.

Clem.

Another notch. Chico dropped.

He calmed the vomit. Licked it back.

Chico hated baths, and this looked like a bath.

Closer into the pool, he saw one that looked like him. A Chihuahua like him. Chico barked.

Another notch.

A drop.

Chico yelped. The machine clicked and moaned.

In the streets, the big cats had taunted him. Led him on with promises of food. "Who's a good boy?"

Before Clem, Chico lived on a chain. Was born on a chain, exploited by an archeologist who had found him and his family in a cave.

Chico was still nursing when he was taken. Aware of the cruelties of the outside, and having Chico as the only survivor of her last litter, his protective mother and siblings attempted to protect their newest addition, but was shot. Chico dreams and hears the yelps of his murdered family, but has never understood.

On the chain where memories start he was starved by the archeologist who belonged to a sect of Nosariis that believe eating the brains of a dead dog would bring one closer to God, but the dog would have to suffer for the enlightenment to work.

The faceless ghost in the robe released Chico, and then he found Clem.

Chico loves Clem.

Soul-sick, Chico barked.

He could feel the bath's lash.

In the streets, the big cats hurt Clem. The big cats weren't so tough; the faceless ghost in the robe hurt them.

Chico's foot was ivory marble, he licked it. The bath was getting closer. He struggled in the harness, and stopped. Chico looked at the one that looked like him at the bottom of the pool. Stone-still, the Chihuahua's eyes were ivory marble.

Chico relaxed, and thought of Clem.

"Who's a good boy?"

Chico's lower-body was submerged in the marble solution. Chico relaxed as his head went under. Chico thought of Clem.

Chico understood love.

•••

The Colonel and a small army of Nosariis made their way to Camp Calico. The goal was to finish them before dawn, because judging by the Militia's recent actions; their next attack would take place at the unveiling of the Imperiam's new lethal chamber.

Two guards in cat masks stood sentinel in front of the fence surrounding the warehouse. The Colonel took them down easily, four double taps from his M-4. As the group entered the base, Calico Militia members in various cat masks rained from all sides with swords, and some with guns. The Nosariis sprayed bullets, without hesitation. The Colonel, unflinchingly led the way, determined to get to the nucleus: Elder Talon.

The cyclopean door of the warehouse creaked open, and up on chains, as if welcoming the Colonel inside. Once through, the door dropped, and snapped shut. The Colonel noticed he was alone, and the warehouse was dark, with no sound, but from the arcade's video and pinball games. A jaundiced spotlight introduced itself revealing Elder Talon with the mask of a tabby, slumped on his throne of rats. Beside him, Nip and Fang, sleek in Siamese cat masks. The concrete floor was painted a checker board, black and red.

The Colonel aimed his weapon, a steady bead on Elder

Talon. Suddenly, the gun clanged to the floor, and the Colonel put a hand to his throat, and came away with blood.

No warning, no sound, a knife was buried in his esophagus. He gagged, and went to his knees. A sound cut the air, and Nip had one foot on the Colonel's head, securing it to the floor.

"Bastards," the Colonel's voice muffled on concrete.

"I'm familiar with your work," said Elder Talon. "The one with the Innsmouth look, a hero to the Imperiam. Why? You're not one of them."

"The Imperiam is home," the Colonel gagged. "Better…why attack our lethal chambers?"

"Ha, ha! There's a new dynasty rising. A child being carried by an unstable vessel, one could say," said Elder Talon.

The Colonel's anguished face twisted with questions.

"HA! HA!" Elder Talon chuckled. "A scion even the emperors of Ulthar are made to bow, and bow they did. While you and these Nosarii remain obedient, like the dogs you are."

Elder Talon slowly rose, and made his way to the Colonel. Fang followed. Nip stepped off of the Colonel's head, and Elder Talon leaned down directly into the Colonel's face. Elder Talon pulled his rubber Tabby mask off, revealing a pallid visage. A mask beneath a mask. The small knife shot from the Colonel's throat, pushed out by hysterical laughter. Nip and Fang removed their masks revealing identical pallid masks. Ghastly, with undistinguished features, and holes for eyes, the three figures simultaneously turned their heads surveying the Colonel.

"HA! HA! HA!" delirium and convulsions. The Colonel writhed on the checker board floor. "Take off the masks! HA! HA! Hail Mother Hydra," the Colonel coughed. "Lay aside your disguises! HA! HA! HA!"

"We. Wear. No. Masks," Elder Talon staccatoed with each word, his voice detached, alien, and guttural.

"No masks? No Masks! HA! HA! HA! HA!"

The three figures seemed to fade into the aether, leaving the Colonel bleeding out on the checker board concrete.

"No masks? No masks!" The Colonel whimpered. "No masks? No masks! No masks? No masks..." On and on until the maroon morning shined through the windows of the warehouse, and onto the old fish-headed man's dying face.

"No mask!" in his death rattles.

•••

"Ah ashes to ashes mama, and sin to sin, every time I hit you, you'll think I've got a dozen hands."

Mac slit his eyes at the maroon morning. The cancerous sun birthing a new day. The notes of the old guitar fretted tight under his clenched toes, his other foot kicking the strings. He sang.

"Give you a punch through that barbed wire fence..."

He could hear the flapping of cloth in the distance, like bat wings. Mac swallowed, nervous. He played on.

"Cause your southern can is mine (every bit of it)..."

Mac moved the nub of his an amputated arm to wipe his brow. The sound was getting closer, and tears birthed in Mac's eyes. One world ends and another begins. He's been through the cycle time and again, but he liked this world. He loved his song. He hoped the Blues existed under the new dynasty, but if they didn't it would be a world without suffering, and hardship. A world without *Blind Willie McTell, Leadbelly, Robert Johnson.*

A world not worth living in, thought Mac.

Before Mac lost his arms he was one of the finest bluesmen in the last dead world. But word spread that he came from a place called Carcosa, and his prowess as a musician was something supernatural. It was said he played prophet and minstrel to a heathen god, a king in yellow.

Mac was lynched by Christians outside of an old blood bucket, hanged and his arms severed to ensure even if he did survive that he would never play the guitar again. Mac persevered and learned to play one song with his feet, and determined to play that song until the next Dynasty. During his recovery he lost everything, but that song.

His eyes closed and he crooned. He looked up and there was a Yellow Knight, surveying him like a curious ghost in its pallid mask and yellow robe. Mac would miss this world, this curb, and the song he played. "*Cause your southern can is mine (in the mornin')...*

The song was the last thing he had to hold on to, and he held on tight to it, twelve strings down with his feet. Mac sobbed for the first time since he could remember. Since the time he was known as Minstrel Mac in worlds long forgotten, his lute long forgotten. A new instrument, a violin, a new song under his feet, sometimes people called him Naked Nubs McMac, DJ Nubs, and sometimes simply, Mac.

Mac lifted his face to the Yellow Knight, and it placed a pallid mask on his face. He cried beneath, emotions interrupting the song. He fretted the neck of the guitar harder, kicked the open strings harder. This always happened when the Dynasty restarted; his life in this world ran through his head. He always missed them.

Familiar faces throwing coins into his guitar case, day in, day out. He never asked for quarter, never has. The imperative was always the song, providing a soundtrack. Food ignored, and the elements on his back. Mac played on.

The Yellow Knight helped Mac to his feet, holding him up as the musician had not stood in aeons.

He noticed a figure in his peripheral, a pregnant belly

in silhouetted in maroon light.

What would this new Dynasty bring to the people he would so miss? He had no idea. He never questioned what he would leave behind. His job was to play until he was called back.

The Yellow Knight helped Mac into a yellow robe. Mac finally gained some balance.

He looked at Chloe's eyeless face.

"Do you have a dollar? Anything to spare?" she said.

Mac let out a howl underneath his pallid mask until the mask became a part of him, and he no longer had eyes to cry with, mouth to sing with, until he wore no mask.

Mac kicked the guitar, and sent it scraping across the concrete to the other side of the street. The song had stopped.

The two Yellow Knights faded into the aether.

"Do you have a dollar? Anything to spare?" Chloe said, and wandered through the maroon morning.

Chapter Thirteen

"ARE YOU OKAY?" ASKED CLEM.

"Do I look okay?" said Cassie. She was catching her breath, sweating. She was deep in the throes of labor, and first in line for the unveiling of the new lethal chamber. Clem was second, and behind them the masses gathered, more than a few in dog masks to show support for the Nosarii.

"Are you sure you want to do this? You'll not only be killing yourself, but the baby, too."

"No shit!" said Cassie, then leaned over, and vomited. She wiped the orange vomit from her lips with her forearm. "It would be crueler to bring this thing into such a world."

"I suppose you're right," Clem sighed.

A giant tarp draped over the chamber, outlining the

black skull design. Beside the chamber, a large podium. Sound techs in assorted dog masks were testing microphones that fed back. The crowd groaned at the noises. "Test. One…two…three…"

Clem surveyed his surroundings. Security was tight, with officers on the podium holding rifles, and officers moving through the crowd. He would either get inside or get shot trying. Worst case scenario would be imprisonment. Clem shuttered at the thought.

The maroon morning had faded to a blue-violet tinge that would soon give way to the purple day.

"Why do you care?" said Cassie.

"I suppose I don't," said Clem.

Cassie wrestled her hand inside the back pocket of her jeans, and took out her cell phone. The numbers for her father's charge cards were saved inside. Her purse had burned up with the Hello Kitty hover car.

"Ohh," Cassie groaned. "I hope they take credit. All I have is daddy's numbers."

Obviously, this girl wasn't from this sector of the

Imperiam. Nobody this young, around here, carried credit cards. Clem felt himself disgusted with this brat.

"Sheer curiosity, but why do you want to die? You're a little young first of all. What are you dying for?" said Clem.

"Ow, ow, ow, ugghh!" Cassie felt pressure release as her water broke. Then the contractions stabbed harder. Clem stepped away from the fluid, causing the crowd to slightly budge. "What am I dying *for*?" Cassie chuckled slightly. "It's none of your business. The fuck are you to question what I am dying for. What are *you* dying *for*? Look at you, what are you anyway," said Cassie. "Some kind of clown?"

This would be the closest thing to a conversation Clem would ever have with another person again, or at least he hoped.

"A mime, actually."

"The fuck?!" Cassie spat. "Aren't mimes supposed to be silent?" Cassie's pain had stabilized, slightly, and she felt mean.

"Sorry," said Clem. "I suppose I'm dying for life itself. Dying for the bad, that outweighs the fleeting good. Dying for the lonely times. Dying for my lost dog. Dying because my father never hugged me…"

"You're a fucking loser," Cassie chuckled.

"Sorry," said Clem, and found himself chuckling a little as well. He couldn't remember the last time he had laughed, and it wasn't ironic that it was upon his reflection. "Basically," said Clem. "I suppose, I'm little different than those mindless Nosarii out there in dog masks dying to support this new suicide chamber, but I suppose they got one over on me. At least they're dying for something substantial."

"There's not anything substantial about this place. The fuck does that even mean?" said Cassie. "Like, look at it. This sector in particular is poor as fuck. I wouldn't live a day here, especially not alone…you know, all pathetic like you," she laughed.

"Sorry we can't all be little rich girls," said Clem.

"That's true," said Cassie. "I may be a little rich girl, but my reasons to be here probably outweigh yours, easily."

"Oh, yeah?" Clem straightened his artificial ears, and crossed his arms. "Do tell?" His condescension was palpable.

"First, the love of my life left this child and me to fend

for ourselves."

"You seem to have money, or at least your daddy does. What's the problem?" said Clem.

Cassie sighed. "Daddy wanted me to get an abortion!"

"You're basically doing that anyway," said Clem.

Frustrated, Cassie rubbed her face. The fuck was this guy, and why was she even talking to him? He had fucked up ears, his mime makeup was all-smudged, and he was ugly as shit.

"Have you ever heard of a place called Carcosa?"

"Yeah, I've heard the name." said Clem. "Why?"

"That's where this baby's father went, and…"

"Seriously?" said Clem, and started laughing.

"Why are you laughing?"

"You do know that's bullshit? Carcosa? It's like Timbuktu, or East Jesus, or Y'ha-nthlei. Just made-up places, myths. Your lover boy is gone." Cassie was crying, and Clem felt bad for belittling her. "It's okay," he reached out, and nervously patted her shoulder. "I personally don't believe in anything. Sorry, that was kind of a dick-thing to say."

Cassie sobbed. "It's okay. Once I get inside here, I won't miss Carl anymore, and that's all that matters."

The day was purple, and the crowd had hushed. The podium was approached by a figure in a red robe, with the mask of a German shepherd. Two Nosariis in the masks of a Chihuahua, and a Poodle stood beside it, arms at the ready. The microphone hissed.

"Brothers and sisters, I present to thee the mighty Imperiam's new lethal chamber!"

A crane moved in close, lowering a hook connecting with a ring on the tarp, and revealing a two-story, marble black skull. Fog machines came on, fireworks ignited the purple sky, and the crowd erupted in cheers and applause.

"This is a monument brothers and sisters to the Nosarii that lost their lives in the name of the Imperiam yesterday. And in the name of independence, from this life, and would not stand for the tyranny of Ultharian terrorists. For twenty-four hours, we were under siege, but still gained our footing. I look upon you masses, some knelt in devotion, and some in the same masks I wear, a face representing obedience, and

servitude to our mighty Imperiam, to our dynasty!"

The crowd had silenced, and all were knelt. Cassie and Clem looked around, and did the same, genuflecting for the speaker.

"Brothers and sisters, I thank you, and I love you. In the name of the Imperiam!"

"THE IMPERIAM!" The crowd let go. Cassie and Clem nervously said the same, and clapped as the crowd went into cheering.

"And I ask, brothers and sisters who will claim their independence from this life?"

The suicide chamber's teeth wrenched open, its eyelids too. One ocular cavity revealed a shirtless, muscular guard in the mask of a Shih Tzu, the other guard of a lean build, and the mask of a Saint Bernard, each with rifles at the ready. Clem gulped. Cassie went for her phone.

"The Imperiam accepts cash, and charge!"

Cassie squealed, and then held her belly when a sharp pain came.

She walked up to feed the numbers to the black skull,

reciting them from her cell phone. Clem took a deep breath, and followed in slowly and awkwardly behind Cassie.

The teeth of the black skull closed after Cassie fed it the numbers. A high-pitched sound went off as it primed.

"Ladies and gentlemen, brothers and sisters," said the speaker and leapt down from the podium with the microphone.

"Young lady, what is your name?"

A sharp pain went off inside Cassie; she grasped her belly, and cried out. "Cassilda Syndrome!"

"Young Miss Syndrome, pregnant too, sacrificing her child as well as herself for the Imperiam!" The crowd cheered.

"And young man, who are you?"

"Clem Castaigne," said Clem.

"You are much too old to be the father of this young lady's child. Did you make a mistake? Is that why you're showing this independence?"

"No," said Clem, and the microphone fed back. The crowd jeered.

"I simply, just want to die."

"And you will, son," the speaker patted Clem's back.

The black skull had primed, and opened its teeth, Cassie started to walk inside.

The crowd parted as a small hunched figure wearing the mask of an orange tabby pulled out an automatic rifle.

"Hail Ulthar!"

Two slight whistles split the air when the guards in the black skull's eyes squeezed off shots. The hunched figure fell to the concrete, and the crowd swarmed around him, and came up with the white mask in celebration.

"Anymore Ultharian doomsayers out there? Ha! Ha! Ha! Ha!"

The crowd laughed along. Cassie stepped inside the black skull, and Clem followed close behind.

"Asshole," said Cassie. "I only paid for one, well two for one, if you count this…" Cassie vomited, "…little bundle of joy."

"I know," said Clem. "Look. I don't have any money. I really want…no, *need* to do this."

"Fuck you," said Cassie, and pushed the button to the

chamber's door for it to close.

"Listen," said Clem.

"Guard!" said Cassie. "This fish-faced fuck is trying to steal a suicide!"

"No, no," said Clem. The crowd behind him hissed, sounded livid. "I'm begging, just let me inside with you. I'll mind my own business. I just want to die, and I'm so broke."

Cassie looked at the poor, ugly guy, his eyes so wanting. She had never done anything nice for anyone, and she was about to leave this fucked up world. Why not?

"Look, um, Cassilda, neither of us will die alone," Clem was kneeled holding her knees, pleading. A bullet hissed past. Clem backed away on his knees, went to the ground, and held his bleeding shoulder.

Cassie looked at Clem, sighed, and stepped out of the suicide chamber.

"It's okay," she said, waving her hands above her head. "I'll pay for him."

Cassie recited more numbers to the black skull, the teeth closed, and the high pitched sound went off as it primed again.

"I'm sorry," said Clem.

"I know," said Cassie.

The crowd behind them booed.

"Brothers and sisters, a testament to camaraderie. Our Imperial friendship! This young lady paid this young man's way inside our lethal chamber. She gave compassion to a thief! I encourage you. If your brother has nothing, then give. Reach deep, and note, inside the chamber is a donations box. Before you pass, reach deep, and give. Hail the Imperiam!

Cassie was panting, "Okay, fish-boy. You ready to do this? You ready to fucking die?"

"Thank you so much," said Clem. "Nobody has ever been this nice to me, ever!"

The suicide chamber had primed, and its teeth came open.

"Brothers and sisters! Our new lethal chamber's first suicide!"

The crowd ignited with clapping, whistles, and cat-calls.

Clem awkwardly took Cassie's hand. She looked at it, then looked up at him, and sighed. Cassie and Clem walked inside the suicide chamber. The black skull's teeth snapped down.

Chapter Fourteen

CASSIE AND CLEM HELD THEIR BREATH INSIDE the suicide chamber. Their eyes stung in the haze of yellow gas, needles on gauges reached the red. Clem gasped.

His head went limp, as well as the hand holding his shoulder where the bullet had entered. Cassie sat beside him, and he started to slowly slump his limp body onto her. She tried to wrestle him off with her elbow.

Her lungs were praying for air, her eyes burned, and she was clenching, holding the child inside her as best she could. She felt some pressure release. The head was crowning, and pushing against the crotch of her jeans. She stood in the small booth, and took her jeans down. The pain briefly succumbed to stark terror when she looked down, and saw the baby had no face. The infant's head was covered in a ghastly white caul. She almost gasped.

The faint sound of the speaker in the German shepherd mask, and muffled cheers came from the crowd outside the suicide chamber.

The yellow gas hissed, and she tried fisting the sting from her eyes. The baby fell out some more, and she kicked Clem's corpse off the bench, and onto the floor.

The child's upper-body was exposed, and upon its shoulder was another head with a ghastly white caul. Her head felt light, but she held her breath.

Outside the sound of the crowd intensified, like close thunder.

The pain, and the misery of the whole situation was becoming too much. She glanced at the cancel button, but decided not to push it. She had come this far, and the thought of living with a child that looked so much like Carl and Lee broke her heart more. Everything since that first night reminded her of Carl, and that's why she was ending her life in the first place, she didn't need this child, day in, day out, reminding her that Carl was gone, and never coming back.

Cassie's bowels let go, the child was completely out, the umbilical cord connected to Cassie. The two-headed child was writhing in a puddle of blood and amniotic fluid next to Clem's corpse on the suicide chamber's floor.

Cassie wanted to breathe, but held it. She kicked her feet like an addict in the throes of Want. She considered the cancel button again.

Outside, the crowd was going into hysteria. The voice of the speaker was gone. Pounding from all around the chamber came from outside, they seem to have gotten to the top of the black skull. The sound of rifles and various firearms were going off.

The fuck is going on?

Cassie noticed the baby still moving. The cauls must be protecting it from the gas. What if the baby lived on after she died?

The suicide chamber was getting hot, an alien-hot. Cassie started to sweat. The suicide chamber was rocking back and forth now. Cassie left her feet when it tipped, her body slammed into the wall adjacent, and Clem's corpse fell on top of her. She tried to push Clem's deadweight off of her, but her strength was long gone. The suicide chamber moved again, and Cassie slammed, this time, on top of Clem. Then, the chamber turned upside-down, and seemed to be flipping, and rolling. From outside came the noise of panic, and fists bashing from all sides of the suicide chamber, even the bottom, and top.

Take a breath, c'mon! Do it!"

The chamber jarred *hard*, and the tools for bludgeoning were released from a console. The heat inside the chamber went from that of a sauna, to something intolerably hellish. The tools for bludgeoning started to prime, and the pitch of the noise from directly inside was so high, and intense, Cassie felt blood dribble down from her ringing ears.

The booth was opaque with yellow. The baby, the controls, the gauges, Clem's corpse, or even her hand in front of her face could not be seen. And the chamber's flipping distorted any sense of direction.

The voices outside became as alien as the heat inside, guttural, and slow, and nothing remotely human.

Breathe!

Cassie calmed herself, and focused.

"I love you Carl," she exhaled, and was met with sunlight.

She was being pulled from the suicide chamber by figures in yellow robes, and pallid masks. She fisted her eyes, but the sun was so hot, so intense, and through her spotty vision, she saw one figure held the two-headed infant toward a blue sky. Cassie's eyes slightly acclimated, and she realized the intensity of the light, and the heat was coming from twin suns.

Carcosa?

All around, the figures bowed around her prone body. From her left, and right making a pathway, and down that pathway, came a figure not unlike the others. This figure had the same pallid mask as the rest, and yellow robe, but this figure had a head upon its shoulder. It held out its hand, and pulled Cassie to a sitting position, and held her. She sobbed on its chest, reached around, and held it in her arms. No sound came from the two-headed figure, not even breathing.

The child was being given to another figure that

swaddled it into a tattered yellow robe, and placed a crown upon the larger head, and a small crown upon the head at the shoulder.

"Carl? Baby, where have you been? Is this the Carcosa your mother was talking about? Am I dead? Why did you leave me!" Anger suddenly flustered Cassie, and the figure held her closer. She continued to sob into its chest. She pounded weakly, and playfully on its arm. "Bastard!"

Down the pathway of the pallid masks kneeling, came a figure with a plate, and a small mound of yellow powder. Cassie recognized it as 'Dalos. She buried her face into the mound and inhaled. She stood, and the figure adorned her in a yellow robe, placed a pallid mask, firmly, on her face, and a jeweled diadem upon her head.

All hail Queen Cassilda!

Chapter Fifteen

TWIN SUNS SANK BENEATH A LAKE AT DUSK. A knight in a yellow robe and pallid mask walked an ocean of corpses in the afterglow of a world that was, and will never be again.

Something white caught its eye, shining between two sprawled bodies in dogs masks.

Interest peaked, and the knight stepped over, around, and on the twisted cadavers, and picked up the shining thing. It was a marble statue featuring a small dog, and seemed to be carved exquisitely, and hyper-realistic. The marble it was carved from seemed warm, almost sentient. The knight would get this artifact to the queen immediately.

The twin suns sank, giving way to black stars. The knight ran through the field of bodies. This statue was an obvious idol of the old world, representing their heathen ways, but he would let the queen decide. The Yellow Queen would make that final judgment.

As the knight ran, under his arm the marble statue seemed to be getting softer. He leapt over the sea of bodies, and made his way to the Queen's court.

Cassie sat upon her throne of bones, a jeweled diadem crowning her fire-red hair. She wore a pallid mask, and yellow robe. She nursed her son, two heads suckling both breasts, and by her side on another throne, her two-headed King. The head at his shoulder slumped, and sleeping.

Below was a legion of her knights, and servants on their knees, some faces to a checkerboard, red and black floor, in humility, and devotion.

Very little was ever spoken in Carcosa, Cassie looked over at her King, and sighed, content.

"Queen!" The Yellow Knight ran into the court, the words guttural, barely decipherable. "Queen! An Idol!"

The excitement caused the court to rise to their feet, and went for their swords, mace, and daggers. Cassie handed the child to the servant, her bared breasts exposed to the Court, uncaring she went for the dagger at her hip.

"Calm the fuck down," said Cassie. "Why are you disturbing my child's feeding?" She motioned to another servant signaling it to bring a plate of 'Dalos. Since she began her reign of Carcosa, the 'Dalos had been to her, and her King a constant companion. The Fourth Dimensional Vortex, their only tether to sanity, and a world long forgotten. The 'Dalos being what separated the Queen and King from the servants.

Carl and Lee rose from their throne unsheathing a sword.

"Beg…beg your pardon," the Yellow Knight stammered.

"Explain yourself!" said Cassie.

"I have…found an idol, my Queen. Something from days forgotten."

"Bring it to me!" Cassie had to lean in closely to make out what the Yellow Knight was saying. The servants, and knight's speech was getting more inhuman every day. Carl and Lee had long since became silent, embracing their destiny in Carcosa, and would simply grunt in regards to positive and negative reactions. Cassie was grateful for this. Carl was cute, but dumb as a rock, and that asshole, Lee? He, or it, was better off mute, as far as she was concerned.

Cassie was too stubborn, and frankly, too lazy to learn Carcosian. She would rather teach her servants her speech, which she knew could be vulgar at times, but she tried to sound more "Queenly" to them as she described it.

The Yellow Knight held the idol up to Cassie. She studied it, closely. The marble felt soft, which would make it easier to destroy.

"This is something those dog worshippers, you know, um worshipped. Why did you bring this before me? That is your King, I am your Queen, and that," she pointed at the child. "Is your prince! To bring this thing to me is so fucking disrespectful!"

The marble was getting malleable. Cassie could feel it…breathing?

Guards went for their swords, ready to kill The Yellow Knight.

Cassie lifted the idol, high above her head, ready to

throw it to the ground, and smash it. The idol started struggling, and under her pallid mask, Cassie's eyes widened. She was holding a dog.

She unmasked, and looked at the dog. It was a Chihuahua, and Cassie started to squeal.

"Look at the cute doggie! Oh my God!"

Chico licked Cassie's face. She held the Chihuahua nuzzled to her neck. "Let him go!"

The Yellow Knight rattled a sigh, and the Court backed away.

"You guys come pet the doggie! Get him some food," said Cassie. The Court scrambled outside, searching for food, and some returned with human limbs.

The Court moved in close, and petted Chico. Cassie put him on the floor, and Chico, instinctively went to gnawing the throne of bones.

"Will you look at him, baby!" said Cassie. Carl grunted.

The servants came back with raw limbs, some human, some not, and put them at the Queen's feet. Chico was starved, and went for an arm.

"He is my pet," Cassie held out her arms, and announced. "He will be treated in the same way you treat your Queen, King, or Prince. He will be fed, and protected. Fuck up and fail to attend the doggie's needs, it's death."

"Hail The Yellow Queen!" The Court cheered.

Chico gnawed the arm. So far, he's seen one familiar face, that girl's, *but the rest of the faces?* Chico wasn't sure what to think. So far, they were nice, but through the stench of corpses outside the Court, he caught Clem's scent faintly on the wind.

Chico couldn't remember the last time he had eaten, it could have been forever ago, it could have been five minutes ago. His time with Clem was forever.

Somewhere under those black stars, his best friend was waiting for him.

END

JASON WAYNE ALLEN has published several short stories, mostly in the Bizarro and Horror genres. Ichthyic in the Afterglow is his first book. Jason Wayne Allen is Southern by the disgrace of some dark god, but currently resides in Mesa, Arizona with his wife and two dogs. He likes Nintendo and beer.

WWW.JASONWAYNEALLEN.WORDPRESS.COM

Also available from ~MorbidbookS~
In Print & Kindle Editions. Available at Amazon.com, CreateSpace.com and Barnes&Noble online.
~click on image for HYPERLINK~

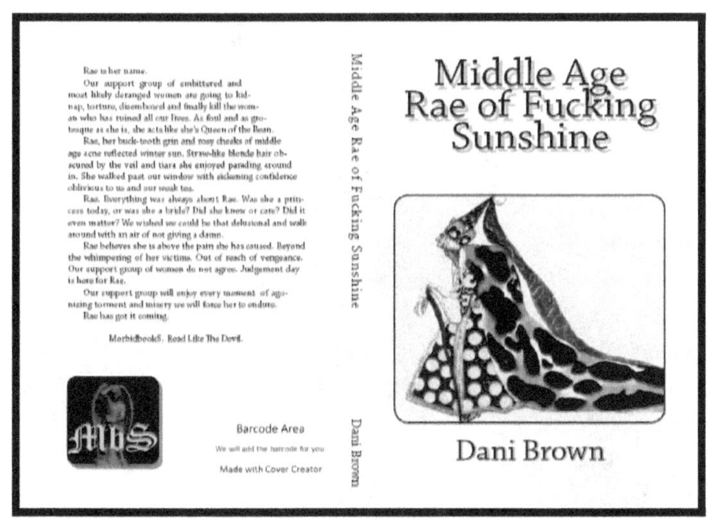

~Rae is her name. Our support group of embittered and most likely deranged women are going to kidnap, torture, disembowel and finally kill the woman who has ruined all our lives. As foul and as grotesque as she is, she acts like she's Queen of the Bean.

Rae, her buck-tooth grin and rosy cheeks of middle age acne reflected winter sun. Straw-like blonde hair obscured by the veil and tiara she enjoyed parading around in. She walked past our window with sickening confidence oblivious to us and our weak tea. Rae. Everything was always about Rae. Was she a princess today, or was she a bride? We wished we could be that delusional and walk around with an air of not giving a damn. Rae believes she is above the pain she has caused. Beyond the whimpering of her victims. Out of reach of vengeance. Our support group of women do not agree. Judgement day is here for Rae.

~Maybe it had started when he was at university.

He had a girlfriend in his final year that had gotten him into some weird stuff sexually then she left him for a guy with a bigger cock. The other guy was some gay looking chump with muscles and a tattoo; the pair had died in a car accident and Brian took a dump on their graves after each of their funerals. Fuck the both of them.

But after she had left him he needed to fill the void of the newfound enjoyment of sickening sexual practices. Brain had purchased one of those 'real life' sex dolls online. Boy did the thing look real; you could bend it into any position and it came armed with enormous tits, willing mouth and a supposedly real feel pussy and anus. The packaging said to 'just add lubricant' but there was a problem. There was something missing; the smells, the tastes and the feel of real skin. You can't emulate that. So Brian set out to attempt to build a real life sex toy made from real life people.

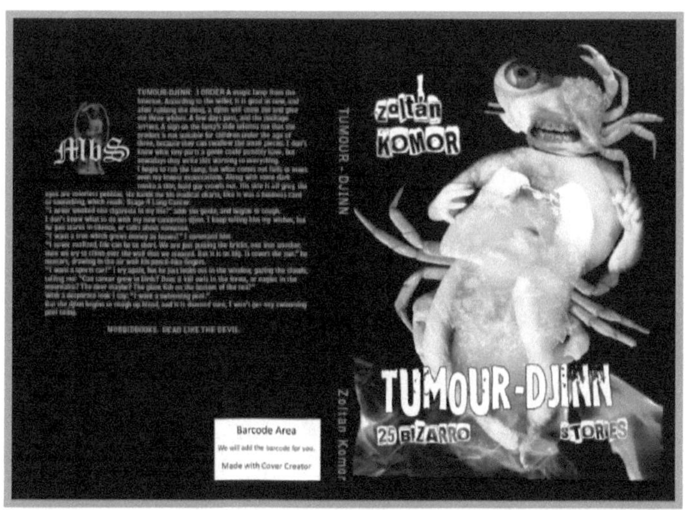

~I ORDER A magic lamp from the internet. According to the seller, it is good as new, and after rubbing the thing, a djinn will come out and give me three wishes. I begin to rub the lamp. Along with some dark smoke a thin, bald guy crawls out. His skin is all grey, the eyes are colorless pebbles.

"I want a tree which grows money as leaves!" I command.

"I never realized life can be so short. We are just putting the bricks, one into another, and then we try to climb over the wall that we created. But it is so big. It covers the sun." he mutters.

"I want a sports car!" I try again, but he just looks out in the window, gazing the clouds, telling me: "Can cancer grow in birds? Does it kill owls in the forest, or eagles in the mountains? The deer maybe? The giant fish on the bottom of the sea?"

With a desperate look I say: "I want a swimming pool."

But the djinn begins to cough up blood....

~Keegan is a late-night public access radio show host, sexual deviant, and militant vegan. He has grown tired of his vegan cause being treated with apathy by the portly, meat-gorging, residents of the small town of Breen Gay, Wisconsin.

The time is ripe for Vegan vengeance.

Keegan harvests roundworms from a local vagrant and mutates them using chemicals stolen from the meat packing plant. He infests the populace with the voracious, parasitic carnivores. Keegan knows that the only way for the people of Breen Gay to eliminate the parasites is to starve them of meat. It is with great expectation that he awaits the oncoming utopia of Veganism.

However, the mutant roundworms will not die easily. The problems for the people of Breen Gay have only just begun.

~FOR SO LONG as anyone could remember, The Flagrant Five have ruled the land with an aggressive hand—enslaving children, destroying the wilderness—but Father Necrocious is tired of it all. One of his worst enemies (and a member of the Flagrant Five), Manservant Genesis, has escaped his imprisonment as a shadow.Therefore, he's enlisted the help of a ragtag group of fabricated Mercenaries to turn the fascists to shadows. The annual Dictators' Ball is pending (a battle in which children are used as pawns to determine the fate of the free world), and the brothers plan to stop the gala before it can commence. As they weave their way through the cartoonish landscape they will fight with their options to either trap the Flagrant Five with their shadow guns, or disobey their creator's orders and finally kill the Five for good.

~The hands of the girls were inside of each-others zip front grey boiler suits and they sat in the blood from where Sonny's face collided with the surface. The brunette had a finger smear of it next to her mouth.

"You two sluts put each other down and go tell Moira that Sonny's done. I'm coming in, just got a little business to attend to first."

As the two started to leave the big blond grabbed the shoulder of the red head and pulled her back.

"Not you Fire-Crotch, all this fucking blood has got me going." She started to unbuckle the belt on her camouflage hot pants.

"Down you go, bitch!"

~Short stories from the Most Depraved Writer in Print. Dark and twisted tales of exquisite violence, rough tricks, narcotics consumption, evil ghosts and drug-snuffling demons. Evil grandfathers and animal-human hybrid clones. Morbid serial killer stalking night darkened hallways of an unsuspecting hospital. Life underground following the frozen apocalypse. Tales of ancient blood-thirsty vampires and Roman decadence. Enjoy all of the hardcore, dystopic, viscerally violent stories. Not for easily offended mamby-pambies. Dark fiction at its finest.

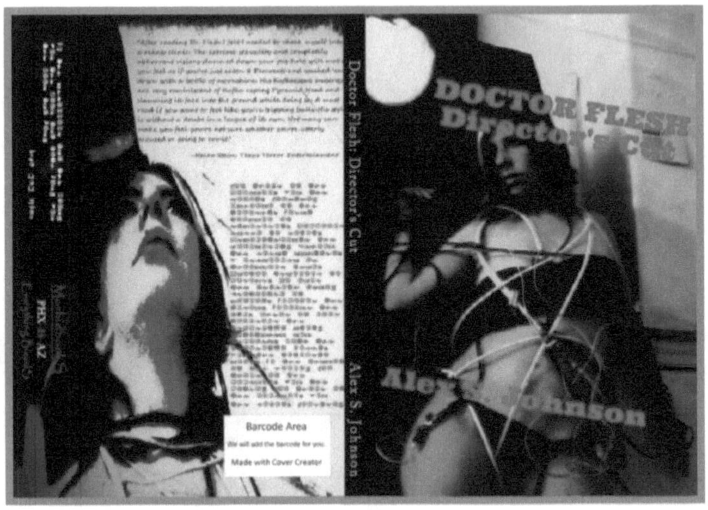

~From Alex S. Johnson, the author of Bad Sunset, Wicked Candy and The Death Jazz, comes a new vision in Bizarro horror. Imagine a TROMA film on meth and acid, one part cyberpunk, one part Franz Kafka, and three parts frankly unsuitable for a sane audience. "Will make you feel as if you've just eaten 8 Percocets and washed 'em down with a bottle of moonshine," says Necro Stein of Texas Terror Entertainment.

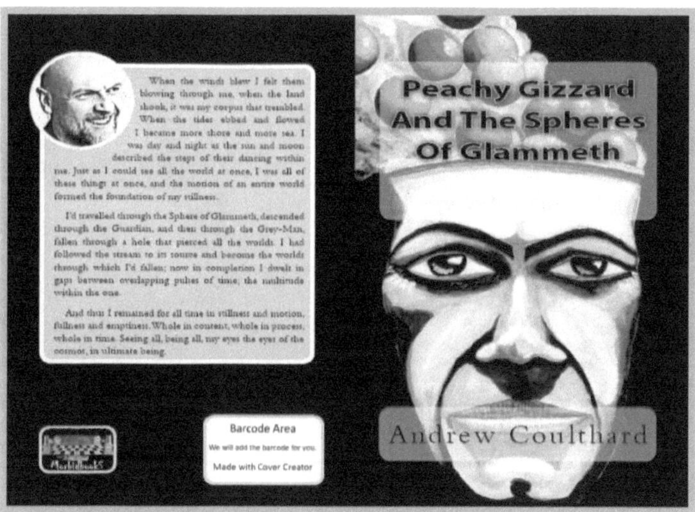

~When the winds blew i felt them blowing through me, when the land shook, it was my corpus that trembled. When the tides ebbed and flowed I became more shore and more sea. I was day and night as the sun and moon described the steps of their dancing within me. Just as I could see all the world at once, I was all of these things at once, and the motion of an entire world formed the foundation of my stillness.

I'd travelled through the Sphere of Glammeth, descended through the Guardian, and then through the Grey-Man, fallen through a hole that pierced all the worlds.

~**He had to have her the moment he saw her trachea ring**. Six months later she was his lovely wife. He performed his duties as a husband and she as a wife. He tolerated a house filled with references to her late first husband and the children they had together. He put up with her prudish ways. He waited. He was patient. He planned. He was adaptable. He was rewarded over the course of a week in her basement. He turned his perverse sexual fantasies of worms and maggots and her lovely crusty trachea ring into a gruesome reality.

~A dirty shameful devil of a secret...

Something that two men share. A legacy that will shock you to your very core. One that is created not out of madness, but of the purest desire. Take a vivid journey into the mind of the killer and his biggest fan. Do you believe in evil? See the knife plunge. Lap at the wounds. Do you still? There is no rational meaning or pretty words that will hide away the darkness that the words of this found journal creates. Inside is the real truth. And it can set you free. Watch all you want. Taste what you dare not have.

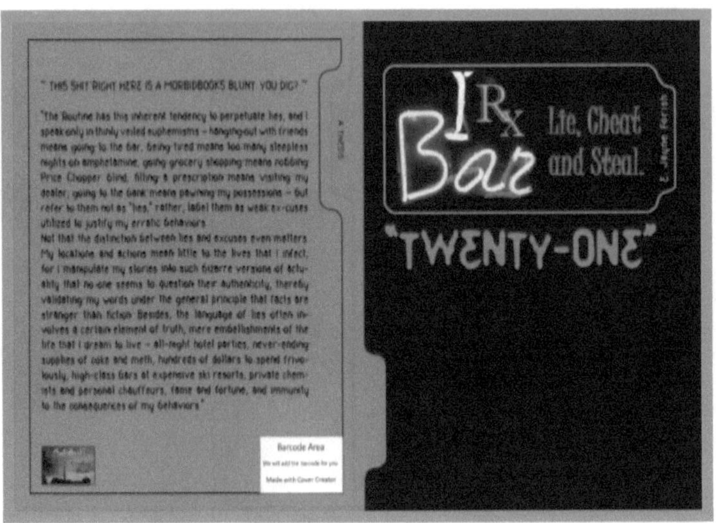

~"The routine has this inherent tendency to perpetuate lies, and I speak only in thinly veiled euphemisms — hanging out with friends means going to the bar; being tired means too many sleepless nights on amphetamine; going grocery shopping means robbing Price Chopper blind; filling a prescription means visiting my dealer; going to the bank means pawning my possessions — but refer to them not as "lies;" rather, label them as weak excuses utilized to justify my erratic behaviours.

~I'm feeling down and dirty, feeling kind of mean, so I give those fans my middle finger. Those poor bastards go nuts. My team looks at me in awe. My coach frowns and the opposing one begins to furiously scratch out new plays. I see our opponents and I almost feel sorry for the poor bastards. Their fans can't help them. Their coach can't help them. I'm going to run them off their own track in front of their own fans and there is not one thing they can do about it.

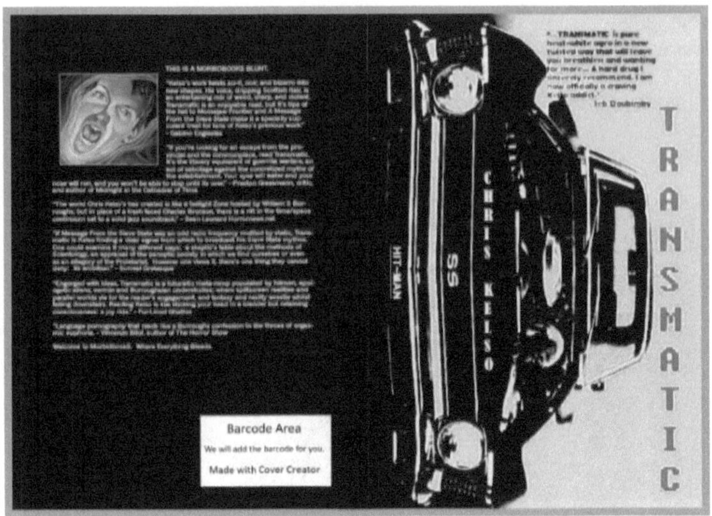

~**"As a part-time hitman/ exterminator, Ignius Ellis's dream is to buy a candy-apple red Nova Supreme.** In the process of trying to earn enough cash to make his dream come true he gets sucked into the rough world of Visitacion Valley, SF. When the tenants in his apartment complex reveal their various extracurricular activities this take an even more bizarre twist and Ellis soon becomes acquainted with the nightmarish Slave State dimension..."

~That's the last time she gets the bigger worm...

Once their flesh flakes away the angels collapse into puddles of hissing goop and withered petals blow into them hurried along by unseen winds. My spit looses its sweet taste to the black flavor of ash. The glowing birds in the bright orange sky burst into small sparkly novas. The sky itself weeps and tears, streaking down like a ruined painting as the dismal grey of life wheezes back before my eyes. I don't blink; praying silently for one last desperate sensation of the high. Lila feels it too. She writhes on the mattress next to me…

~Scary as ever.

He looked at her and grinned wickedly, the overcasting shadows of the outer corner of the stone wall, combined with the flickering light above them, created a deadly feature across the side of his face. He sees her lying helpless. He chuckled eerily, and instantly raised his hand. Her eyes widened to the sight of the gleaming sharp knife in his grasp. He even held it up for her to see it better.

She stared up at him and then to the knife, panting in fear. Her heart pounded throughout her body as he chuckled once more saying deeply,

"Oh excellent. I've found you . . ."

~Within these twisted and perverted pages, Johnson manages to demolish clichés with a jaded finesse that I've personally never encountered in written form. Another apparent talent is his effortless deconstruction of pop-culture allegories and references as found in his story "Vampussy." No one is safe or spared from his dagger sharp sarcasm and wit.

While not without its flaws, my appreciation for this kind of talent and voice is what made his writing so fun to read, even if he might possibly be out of his ever-loving mind.

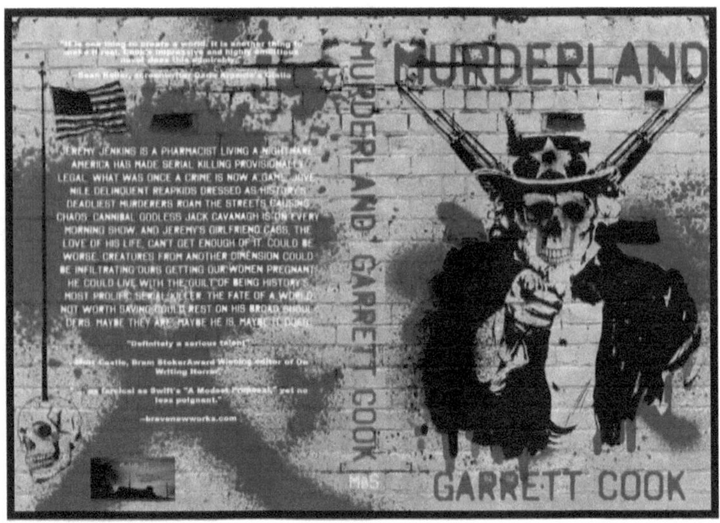

~In Garrett Cook's Murderland serial killers are idolized by society. Their deeds are followed obsessively by television pundits and the adoring public. A subculture has grown up around this phenomena, called "Reap." Laws are created to allow this activity to flourish, including designated "safe zones' where killers can practice their trade without fear of persecution. Fans of the top rated serial killers celebrate each new kill on social media and television. Programs glorify their deeds.

The culture of Murderland is violent and mirrors our own violent society and its decadent obsessions.

~Born whole from the rectum of a dying patient, Morbid silently stalks the hospital's hallways, heinously dispatching the most helpless of patients and in the most painfully repulsive of manners. In the meantime, in order to pay for his family and home that includes his ghost step-father Sammy and his pet aborted fetus Chip, Westphal has to ingest mounds of dangerous narcotics to get through his night shifts. Barely hanging on to his Care Tech gig by his fingernails, the last thing Westphal needs is to be accused of Morbid's evil deeds. You, on the other hand, simply seek some solace from all Your diseases.

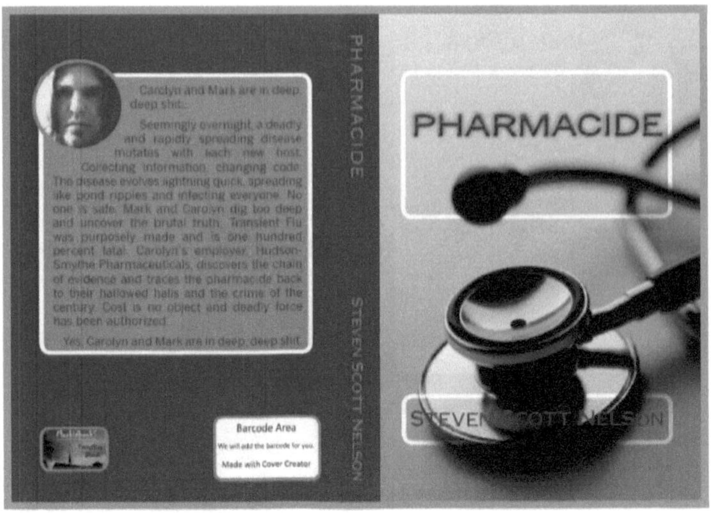

~It looks like Carolyn and Mark are in deep, deep shit... Mark and Carolyn live in an alternate 1989 where Ronald Reagan is on his fourth presidential term. The USA has a rigid, long-standing caste system and abortions were never made legal. Being homeless is a crime that is punishable by imprisonment in Tent City. Most of Mark's ER patients are inmates at this camp and are victims of a new disease dubbed: Transient Flu. This deadly and rapidly spreading disease mutates with each new host, collecting information, changing code. The disease evolves lightning quick, spreading like pond ripples…

~IMMANUEL THE CHRIST has some nerve. Jonah has already lost everyone he loves to Pilate the vampire and his Harbor drug violence. Jonah now trudges through his days staying as high on Plata as possible. He just wants to be left alone while he waits for his turn to die. The Christ has other plans for him. She sends Pedro, to assign Jonah to order the Herod to dismantle the Harbor's Plata trade. Jonah decides to run. But you can't run from God. As Jonah learns the hard way when the 'Edmund Fitzgerald' goes down in rough seas, with the reluctant prophet on board…

~Five Very Wicked Shorts. Brought to you with love and blood from The Grim Reverend Steven Rage, the 'Most Depraved Writer in Print'. ~

Through the sheer shock of his presentation, Rage forces readers to consider the alternatives, to look at the garbage in the streets, to see what is swept into the gutters at night right before all decent people awake to see another cleaned up version of the day. Depravity at its finest, but really the stories are loads of fun.

~Pontius Pilate is cursed to be a vampire. Life after life after life.~ And for the Plata dealing Pilate, his life is more like a death sentence. His only chance surviving is to keep on selling his monthly quota of Plata. This new man-made narcotic is a potent speed-ball designed to amp up the user, while also numbing the conscience into euphoric oblivion. To nullify the pain. To stifle the torture. To run and to hid from all the anguish inside. PILATE is a drug lord vampire in this re-telling of Christ's final days.

~So I, The Spun Monkey, have returned from running my errands, safe and sound. Having failed rehab once again, The Spun Monkey went ahead and procured myself an 8-ball of crispy, crunchy Columbian Bam-Bam. I chipped, chopped, lined and blasted off with two bigguns up each side. OOH OOH EEE EEE-fuckmerunning- OOH-OOH-OOH, motherfuckers! Monkey be ready... Yes, indeeeeeed.... Having had my jet fuel, I then sat my hairy asshole down at the keyboard and began flailing away. The monkey hopes you dig the fruits of my labors in 'The Spun Monkey's Digest'. And if you not ... well then ... you can go eff yourself, Capitan!

~Following religious folklore, parables, and beliefs, Rage presents the readers with a God who truly is the Shepherd that leaves no sheep behind. While this tale is deeply woven with the intricacies of a dark, drug-infested world ruled by evil forces, this is the story of a lost sheep. All are God's children, even the most foulest of evil creatures who by their own will have become so through their spiritual and physical copulation with the Devil, and as such, in God's mercy, still are given a chance to be saved.

~ CARGO CONTAINS: ~

Space-wrecked on Venus by Neil R. Jones

For All the Marbles by Rev. Steven Rage

Tony and the Beetles by Philip K. Dick

Acid Bath by Vaseleos Garson

The Butterfly Kiss by Arthur Dekker Savage

The Moon Destroyers by Monroe K. Ruch

From some of the giants of the Golden Age to the darkest of dystopian noir, MorbidbookS SciFi Anthology will take you from hopeful space travel to living hand-to-mouth in the despair beneath the Earth.

Welcome to your future.

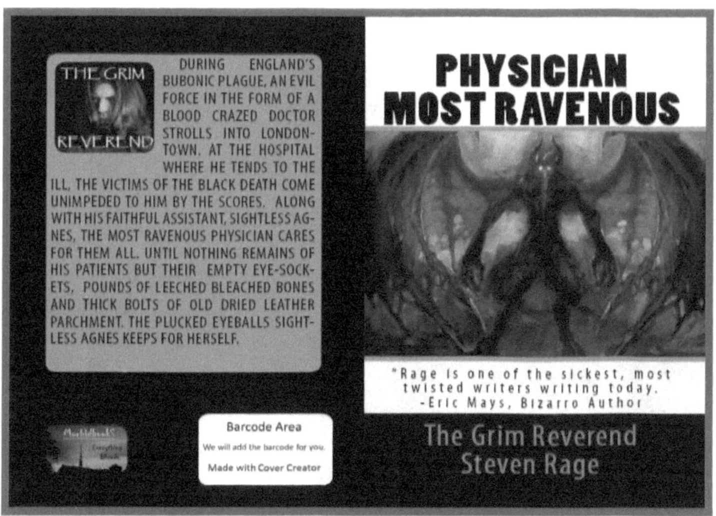

~During the height of England's Bubonic Plague an ancient Evil Force strolls into London-Town in the form of a would-be doctor. It could smell the blood from miles away, wanting only to help. At the hospital where he cares for the victims of this Black Death, the ill come to him unimpeded. They arrived and fell by the scores. With the help of his ever-faithful assistant, Sightless Agnes, a most ravenous cares for them all. Eating his way through an entire hospital, he treats them until there is nothing left. Nothing save their empty eye sockets, a few pounds of leeched bleached bones and some bolts of old dried-out flesh-leather parchment.

~New from MorbidbookS: Where Everything Bleeds is an instant collector's specimen and a certain stunner. ~ Be the first freak on your block to acquire this singular and unexpurgated exquisite culling of The Grim Reverend Steven Rage's favorite 'meds'. Enjoy this one-of-a-kind vivid look into the twisted mind of The Most Depraved Writer In Print as he captains you through the intoxicating stain of his wicked imagination. Included are numerous Photos, Paintings and Illustrations embellished with dramatic grayscale that enhance these iniquitous and magnificent Dark Fantasy fables…

~This was the other side of the killer clown, the one he hid, the dark side. Publically, the man loved and craved the laughter and applause of children. He delighted in playing his character for them and ate up the love that they gave him. He mugged for them. He danced and pranced around the ring, getting them to clap along with him as he performed his tricks and stunts. His patented pratfalls brought gales of laughter. But as much as he craved the laughter of children, he also craved the cries and screams of women as they submitted to his own particular brand of sadism. He wielded a whip better than any lion tamer in the business. It thrilled him to watch the firm young flesh of a woman writhe and twist in delicious agony as his ropes bit deeply into them and his crops left myriads of latticework markings on their bodies. Their anguish was his delight.

Read Like The Devil.
MbS
MbS
MorbidbookS

www.ingramcontent.com/pod-product-compliance
Lightning Source LLC
Chambersburg PA
CBHW021114130626
46554CB00002B/689

* 9 7 8 0 6 9 2 3 2 1 1 2 6 *